CW00859929

Mama's Hats

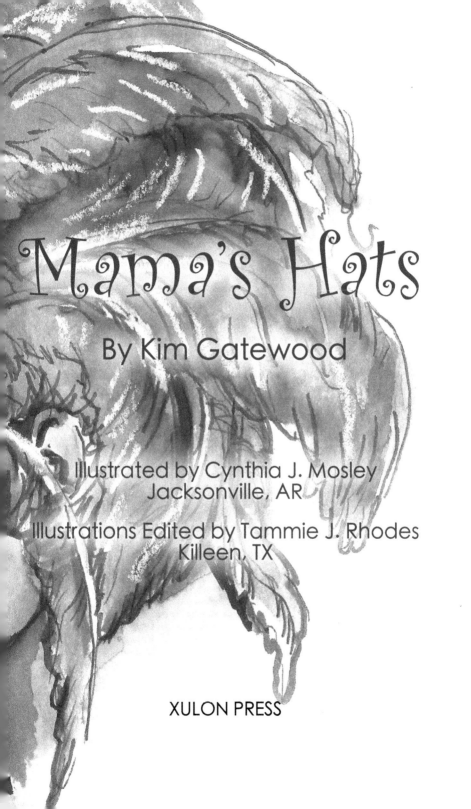

Mama's Hats

By Kim Gatewood

Illustrated by Cynthia J. Mosley
Jacksonville, AR

Illustrations Edited by Tammie J. Rhodes
Killeen, TX

XULON PRESS

Xulon Press
2301 Lucien Way #415
Maitland, FL 32751
407.339.4217
www.xulonpress.com

Paperback ISBN-13: 978-1-66283-057-0
Hard Cover ISBN-13: 978-1-66283-058-7
Ebook ISBN-13: 978-1-66283-059-4

Scripture quotations are taken from

THE NEW KING JAMES VERSION.

In honor and dedication to my mother, Annette Zackery.
Rest in heaven, Mom. I love you!

"ALL ABOUT MAMA!"

Mama loves hats!

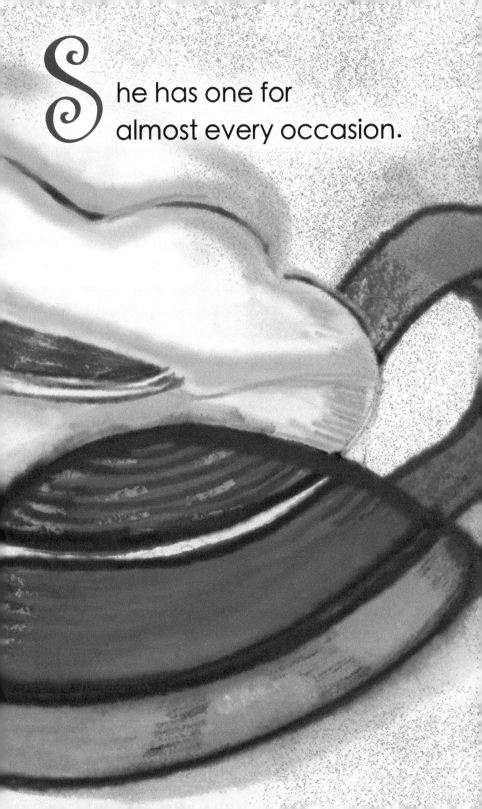

She has one for almost every occasion.

Big hats, tall hats, furry hats, and even small hats.

Mama has hats in almost every color:

red ones, green ones, and yellow ones too!

She has orange ones,
pink ones, and different
shades of blue!

Mama's hats are
so special that
every time she places
one on her head...

Off we go on one of her zany adventures, faster than a thoroughbred! SHAZAM!

With a chef hat in hand, on her head it goes. KERPLUNK!

Chef Luige appears,
with Italian meatballs
up to her nose!

Taking brother and I to school, Mama does it with flair.

I nstantly, she becomes stock car racer 00, as the wind blows back her hair. WEE!

Mama pretends it is Sunday almost every day of the week!

She especially enjoys wearing her church hat because through the feathers, she loves to peek. BOO!

On snowy days, Mama loves to wear her toboggan and her mittens with just the thumbs.

Instantly, we are at the Winter Olympics, skiing down a giant slalom. WHOOSH!

With Mama,
rainy days
are never blue.

She sails through dangerous waters, Yellow-beard and her pirate crew. ARGHH!

On sunny days when things are very hot and icky...

Mama wears her military beret and carries her super-soaker to spray away the sticky. ZAP!

I love Mama's hats and all the adventures they bring. They allow us to spend time together, and makes us feel as if, WE CAN DO ANYTHING!

Philippians 4:13 – "I can do all things through Christ who strengthens me." (NKJV)

CPSIA information can be obtained
at www.ICGtesting.com
Printed in the USA
LVHW071645131021
700347LV00004B/86